THE BOXCAR

MOUNTAIN TOP MYSTERY

Time to Read® is an early reader program designed to guide children to literacy success regardless of age or grade level. The program's three levels correspond to stages of reading readiness, making book selection straightforward, and assuring that when it's time for a child to read, the right book is waiting.

Level 1 — Beginning to Read

- Large, simple type
- Basic vocabulary
- Word repetition
- Strong illustration support

Level 2 — Reading with Help

- Short sentences
- Engaging stories
- Simple dialogue
- Illustration support

Level 3 — Reading Independently

- Longer sentences
- Harder words
- Short paragraphs
- Increased story complexity

Library of Congress Cataloging-in-Publication data is on file with the publisher.

Copyright © 2021 by Albert Whitman & Company
Hardcover edition first published in the United States of America
in 2021 by Albert Whitman & Company
Paperback edition first published in the United States of America
in 2021 by Albert Whitman & Company
ISBN 978-0-8075-5289-6 (paperback)
ISBN 978-0-8075-5290-2 (ebook)

THE BOXCAR CHILDREN® is a registered trademark
of Albert Whitman & Company.

TIME TO READ® is a registered trademark
of Albert Whitman & Company.

Printed in China
10 9 8 7 6 5 4 3 2 1 RRD 26 25 24 23 22 21

Cover and interior art by Liz Brizzi

Visit The Boxcar Children® online at www.boxcarchildren.com.
For more information about Albert Whitman & Company,
visit our website at www.albertwhitman.com.

THE BOXCAR CHILDREN®

MOUNTAIN TOP MYSTERY

**Based on the book by
Gertrude Chandler Warner**

Albert Whitman & Company
Chicago, Illinois

"I want to climb a mountain!"
said Benny Alden.
Jessie smiled at her
little brother.
"You've had too much sugar.
Mountain climbing
is hard work."
"I mean it!" Benny said.
"Can we, Grandfather?"
Henry, Jessie, Violet, and Benny
had hiked many times.
But never up a mountain.
Grandfather rubbed
his mustache.
"I know just the place," he said.

The Aldens loved adventures.
For a little while they had even
lived in a boxcar in the forest.
It had been their home.
They'd had all kinds of
adventures in the boxcar.

Then Grandfather found them.
Now the children had
a real home.
And they still had all kinds of
adventures together.

The Aldens took a long drive.
When they stopped, there
were mountains all around.
One had a big, flat top.
"That one should be called…"
Benny thought of the right
words. "Flat Top!"
"That is just what it is called,"
a smiling woman said.
"This is my friend,
Dr. Osgood,"
Grandfather explained.
"She looks for fossils
in the area."

"It's a long hike up Old Flat Top," said Dr. Osgood. "Keep your eyes open. You might find a treasure!"

Dr. Osgood was right.

The hike was long.

"Who knew mountain climbing took so much…"

Benny sat down.

He thought of just the right word.

"Climbing!"

"Maybe there's another way up," said Violet.

But Grandfather shook his head.

There was only one trail.

Benny took a bite of chocolate.

"Okay, I'm ready again."

The long hike was worth it.
Old Flat Top was not the
tallest mountain, but it had
the best view.

"I don't think those trees have ever been cut down," said Violet. "That's right," said Grandfather. "No one lives for miles around."

After exploring Old Flat Top,
the children started down.
Benny led the way.
Hiking was easier on
a full stomach.
But when Benny took a step,
the rocks tumbled away!

The trail was gone.
The Aldens could not
get down.
They would have to wait for
Dr. Osgood to send help.

The Aldens set up camp.
The town glowed far away.
Then Violet saw another,
lonely light down below.

Was someone living in the forest?

In the morning, the children
woke up to a loud noise.
It was Dr. Osgood!

As they all flew away,
Violet looked back at the
strange, flat mountain.
She saw another strange thing.
Where the trail had been,
there was a big hole.
Was there a cave in the
mountain?

"I am *so* hungry," Benny said
at lunch, "but I'm sad too.
Our adventure is over."
"Maybe not," said Violet.
She told them about
the lonely light and the hole
in the mountain.
"I wonder what's inside,"
Henry said.
"Can we stay and find out?"
Grandfather rubbed
his mustache.
"I think this adventure is just
getting started!"

First, the Aldens went
deep into the forest.
They met a woman named
Lovan in a little house.
Her family had lived there
for many, many years.
"Everyone else has moved
away," Lovan said.
"I am the last one here."

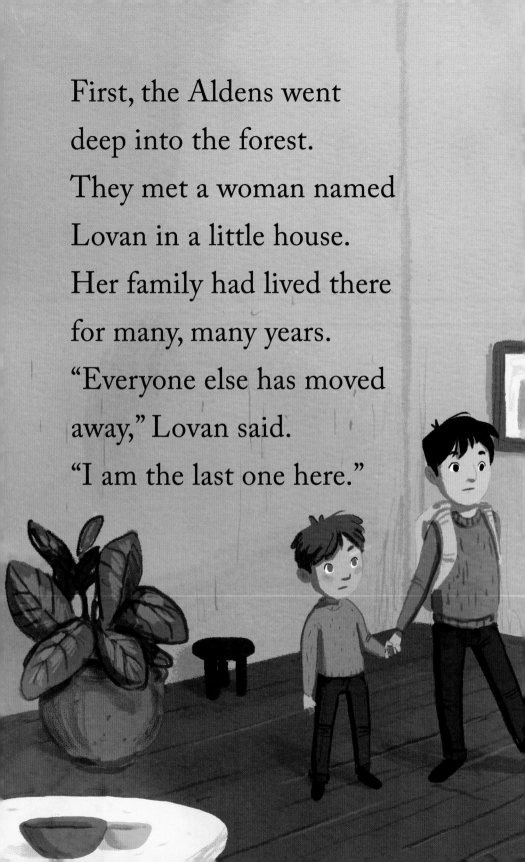

The Aldens felt bad that
Lovan was all alone.
Still, Violet asked her
a question.
"We saw a cave in the
mountain. Do you know
anything about it?"

Lovan told them a story.

Years ago, people had tried to move her family off the land.

Her grandfather hid valuables in a secret place in the mountain.

But no one knew where.

"I'm afraid they have been lost," Lovan said.

Benny looked up at the hole in the mountain.

"Maybe we can help you!" he said.

Benny didn't need any
chocolate to hike up
Old Flat Top this time.
But when they got to the cave,
it was not yet safe to go in.
"Years ago, a rockslide covered
this cave up," Dr. Osgood said.

"The rockslide is how Old
Flat Top got its flat top.
Benny, your rockslide opened
the cave back up!"

Workers cleared rocks to make the cave safe.

The children couldn't wait to explore it.

"Do you think we might find treasure?" asked Henry.

Dr. Osgood held up a fossil. "I found some already!"

"We are looking for another kind of treasure," said Henry.

But hunting for any treasure would have to wait.

A big storm was on the way. The Aldens hiked down.

When Dr. Osgood came down,
she was all wet.
She had not gone in
the cave yet.
"But there was something
strange," she said.
"A young man came up.
He wanted to look in the cave."

Was someone else looking for the treasure?

That night, the children
fell asleep right away.
They wanted to wake up early
to look for Lovan's treasure.
But Benny woke up too early.
Much, much too early.
He heard a noise outside and
looked out the window.
A young man went into the
next motel room.
Was it the same man from
the mountain?

The next day, the children
hurried up Old Flat Top.
They hoped they weren't
too late to find the treasure.
Dr. Osgood led them
into the cave.

"Look at this!" she called.

"Is it Lovan's treasure?"

asked Benny.

Dr. Osgood held up a rock.

Benny sighed.

Maybe someone else *had*

already been there.

Then Benny saw
a strange stone.
It was shaped like a square.
And when he picked at it…

"The treasure!" said Violet.

"It's from Lovan's grandfather!"
Jessie said.

"She will be so happy."

"Did you say Lovan?"
a voice asked.
The children spun around.
Benny knew the young man.
He had seen him
the night before!

"You know Lovan?"
asked Jessie.
The boy was named David.
"I never met her," he said.
"But she was my great-aunt.
When I heard about the cave,
I came to find our
family's treasure.
I am surprised it is here!"
"We have another surprise,"
said Jessie.
"Lovan is still alive!"

There was only one thing
left to do.
The Aldens went into the
forest, where Violet had seen
the lonely light.

"My grandfather's things!"
said Lovan.
"You found my family treasure!"
"We found something else too,"
said Benny.
He thought
of just the
right words…

"The treasure of family!"

Keep reading with The Boxcar Children®!

Henry, Jessie, Violet, and Benny used to live in a boxcar. Now they have adventures everywhere they go! Adapted from the beloved chapter book series, these early readers allow kids to begin reading with the stories that started it all.

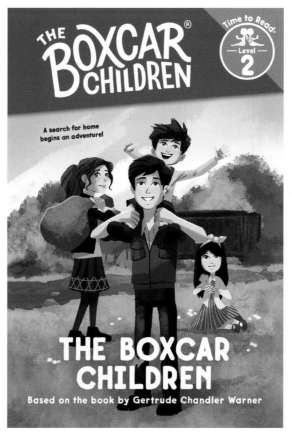

HC 978-0-8075-0839-8 · US $12.99
PB 978-0-8075-0835-0 · US $4.99

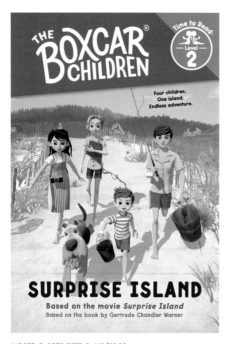

HC 978-0-8075-7675-5 · US $12.99
PB 978-0-8075-7679-3 · US $4.99

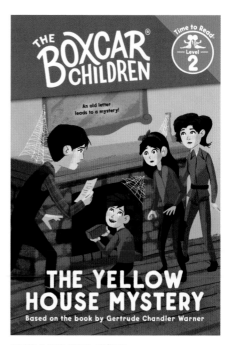

HC 978-0-8075-9367-7 · US $12.99
PB 978-0-8075-9370-7 · US $3.99

HC 978-0-8075-5402-9 · US $12.99
PB 978-0-8075-5435-7 · US $3.99

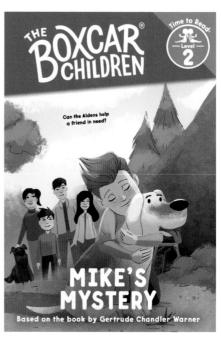

HC 978-0-8075-5142-4 · US $12.99
PB 978-0-8075-5139-4 · US $3.99

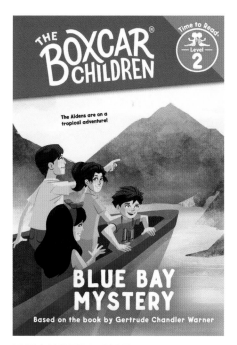

The Aldens are on a tropical adventure!

BLUE BAY MYSTERY
Based on the book by Gertrude Chandler Warner

HC 978-0-8075-0795-7 · US $12.99
PB 978-0-8075-0800-8 · US $3.99

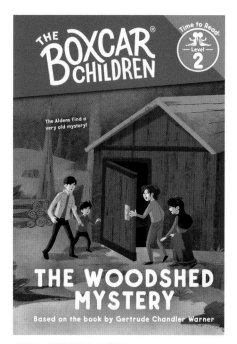

The Aldens find a very old mystery!

THE WOODSHED MYSTERY
Based on the book by Gertrude Chandler Warner

HC 978-0-8075-9210-6 · US $12.99
PB 978-0-8075-9216-8 · US $3.99

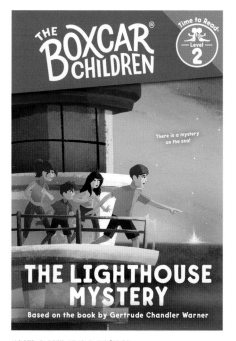

There is a mystery on the sea!

THE LIGHTHOUSE MYSTERY
Based on the book by Gertrude Chandler Warner

HC 978-0-8075-4548-5 · US $12.99
PB 978-0-8075-4552-2 · US $4.99

GERTRUDE CHANDLER WARNER discovered when she was teaching that many readers who like an exciting story could find no books that were both easy and fun to read. She decided to try to meet this need, and her first book, *The Boxcar Children*, quickly proved she had succeeded.

Miss Warner drew on her own experiences to write the mystery. As a child she spent hours watching trains go by on the tracks opposite her family home. She often dreamed about what it would be like to set up housekeeping in a caboose or freight car—the situation the Alden children find themselves in.

While the mystery element is central to each of Miss Warner's books, she never thought of them as strictly juvenile mysteries. She liked to stress the Aldens' independence and resourcefulness and their solid New England devotion to using up and making do. The Aldens go about most of their adventures with as little adult supervision as possible—something else that delights young readers.

Miss Warner lived in Putnam, Connecticut, until her death in 1979. During her lifetime, she received hundreds of letters from girls and boys telling her how much they liked her books.